SETNA'S JOURNEY

By

Richard Brown

First published in 2001
by Anglia Young Books
Anglia Young Books is an imprint of MILL PUBLISHING
PO Box 55
4 Balloo Avenue
Bangor
Co. Down BT19 7PJ

Illustrations by Robin Lawrie

British Library Cataloguing-in-Publication Data

A catalogue record for this book is available
from the British Library

ISBN 1 871173 63 9

Printed in Great Britain by
Ashford Colour Press, Gosport, Hampshire

SETNA'S
JOURNEY

Author's Note

This story takes place during the reign of King Seti I (1294-1279) during the 19th dynasty of the New Kingdom - that is, over three thousand years ago. The first and third sections occur in a town on the great river Nile south of the city of Thebes. The middle section happens in Thebes itself, at the temple complex known as Karnak, when King Seti's son, the future Rameses II, was ten.

Setna is the son of a wealthy court artist and farmer. He is one of the fortunate few who were

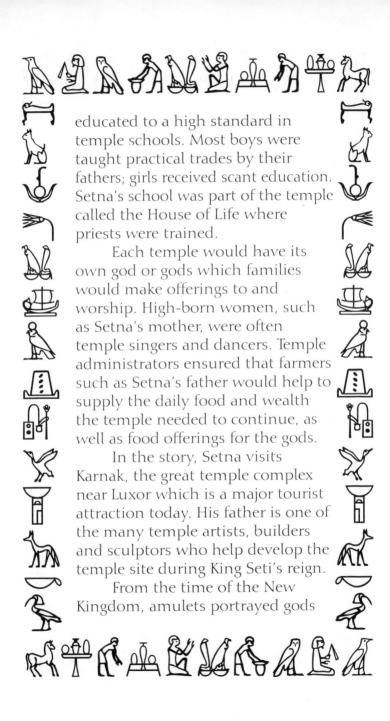

educated to a high standard in temple schools. Most boys were taught practical trades by their fathers; girls received scant education. Setna's school was part of the temple called the House of Life where priests were trained.

Each temple would have its own god or gods which families would make offerings to and worship. High-born women, such as Setna's mother, were often temple singers and dancers. Temple administrators ensured that farmers such as Setna's father would help to supply the daily food and wealth the temple needed to continue, as well as food offerings for the gods.

In the story, Setna visits Karnak, the great temple complex near Luxor which is a major tourist attraction today. His father is one of the many temple artists, builders and sculptors who help develop the temple site during King Seti's reign.

From the time of the New Kingdom, amulets portrayed gods

and goddesses, as well as animals and other symbols. There were two kinds of amulets - those worn for daily protection, and those used as part of the mummification and burial process. Setna wears an ankh symbolising eternal life, and he has two other amulets, one representing the god of the Nile floods, Hapy (or Hapi) and another of the goddess Ma'at, representing justice and balance in life. He firmly believes in their power to protect him against evil and misfortune.

Egyptian children, particularly boys, would have their heads shaven except for a single plait called a sidelock, which features in the hieroglyph for 'child'. When they were about to become teenagers, the sidelock would be cut off and their hair would be allowed to grow. This was an important stage in growing-up, and boys like Setna would look forward to it.

PART ONE
AKHET: THE NILE FLOOD

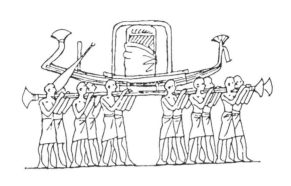

'Egypt is a gift of the Nile.'

How many times had Setna heard that? His wet-nurse had taught him the saying before he could walk. His teacher, Siamun, had made sure that all the schoolboys in his charge understood that everyone depended on the flooding of the great river each year. Without the *inundation*, as they called it, Egypt would be nothing more than wind and burning sand.

'Good news!' Siamun shouted, entering the classroom. 'The priests declare that Sirius the dog-star is bright at last. He heralds the coming of the waters.'

Siamun continued. 'The floods are late this year. But the priests have seen the signs in the heavens at last. The waters are flowing down to us. We must all go to the temple and make offerings to the god Hapy.'

The boys scrambled to their feet. They had been waiting for this for weeks.

'Remember,' Siamun warned, 'we are going to enter the house of the gods. It is where they live and breathe and watch over our affairs.'

Chattering excitedly, the boys filed out of the House of Life, where they were taught to be scribes, to make their way towards the great temple. Usually they looked to see what was going on in the workshops, granaries, animal pens, food shops and dwellings that surrounded the school, but today they thought only of the celebrations.

Outside the great gateway to the temple, the people from the town had already gathered. They had been idle since the harvesting of last year's crops, and were looking forward to planting this season's crops in the rich silt left behind by the Nile floods.

Setna noticed his younger sister, Tiy, among the crowds outside. She was clutching the hand of her nurse. Tiy scowled at him, jealous of his freedom.

The first court was crowded too. People were drawing water from the wells and handing it around in goblets. In the second court, where only the most important families were allowed, Setna saw his mother. She wore a long, thin robe, a bright beaded collar and feathers in her hair. She was part of the temple choir of women who sang and danced at festivities, rattling sistrums above their heads.

Siamun chose half a dozen boys from his class to enter deeper into the temple and Setna was one of them! It would be the first time he'd ever entered one of the inner chapels. His parents would be proud of him. And Tiy would be even more jealous!

White-robed and shaven-headed priests washed the boys' hands and feet to purify them.

Setna felt dwarfed by the huge columns in the inner halls, carved with pictures of plants. On the ceiling golden stars had been painted.

'I must give thanks to the god Hapy,' he thought, closing his eyes for a second. For several nights he had prayed to the god Hapy to flood the great Nile.

Carrying offerings of food, the boys filed
into the chapel where the stone-carved god
loomed high on a plinth. His pot-belly

suggested plenty. On his head were carved plants of the river. The boys bowed and gave their offerings - fruit, bread, honey, wine - to a priest who set them around the god.

'They say Hapy, when he isn't here, lives in deep, dark caverns,' Setna whispered to the boy beside him.

The thought of the god sometimes frightened him. What if he was angry with his people and withheld the flood? They would all die of hunger, or perish at the hands of their enemies as they tried to escape across the desert.

The following day the whole town went down to the water's edge to watch the Nile rise and widen as the waters flowed from Lower Egypt.

Setna was keeping his family waiting. He was searching for an amulet his father had given him last year, representing the god Hapy.

'I wore this when I was a boy,' his father had said. 'My father gave it to me. So treasure it, my son, and wear it at the next inundation.'

Impatiently, Setna shouted for Khefre, their Nubian servant-boy. Khefre had been brought back from a campaign in Nubia where his parents had been killed in a raid on his village. Setna's father had taken pity on the fine-looking boy and had bought him to work as a servant in the house.

'Khefre, you know the amulet of Hapy I showed you? I can't find it anywhere, and I must wear it today.'

Khefre said nothing.

'Well, aren't you going to look for it?' Setna said, raising his voice.

Khefre was two years older than Setna, handsome, black, his hair falling in curls to his neck. It was the servant-boy's full head of hair which annoyed Setna most. Like all the boys of his age or younger, Setna had to wear his hair to one side in a plait, while the other side was shaved. It made him feel a boy still, not the strong, brave, independent youth which he yearned to be. How he longed to grow a full head of hair like Khefre's!

Sullenly, Khefre looked for the amulet while Setna stood by, fuming.

'I can't see it anywhere,' Khefre said. The servant-boy had a faint smile on his face.

'You know where it is, don't you?' Setna accused him, giving voice to his annoyance. 'You've hidden it somewhere, haven't you?'

Khefre frowned. 'Of course I haven't!'

Setna was about to accuse him again, when he noticed his father standing in the doorway.

'We are waiting,' Salitas said quietly.

Setna flushed. It was wrong to shout at the servant-boy in that way, wrong to accuse him without proof. Now his father would be disappointed in him, for it was against their belief to treat anyone with disrespect, especially in one's own house.

The family - his parents in fine ceremonial dress, his sister Tiy, her nurse and some household staff - joined the procession from the temple. Sacred barks, in the shape of Nile boats, were carried aloft by the priests. In each bark was a statue of a god. The god Hapy led the procession in the first bark. The gods were covered, for most people were not allowed to look upon their likeness.

His family split. Setna's mother joined the women of the temple, to sing and dance. His father stayed with the priests and scribes and temple officials who carried the sacred barks. Setna was not too pleased to be left with Tiy and her nurse.

The nurse suddenly saw some of her relatives in the crowd ahead of her. 'Look, there's my sister,' she exclaimed excitedly, 'and my aunt. Oh, and Grandfather too. They have come from the fields up-river. Oh, Master Setna, I haven't seen them for a whole year. May I join them?'

'You can't take Tiy with you,' Setna said.

'Oh, thank you!' she exclaimed, joyfully. She handed over Tiy and was gone before Setna could protest that that was *not* what he had meant!

'Come back!' Tiy shouted after her nurse.

'Be quiet!' Setna demanded. 'Behave yourself.'

Tiy scowled. But then she realised it might be fun to spend the day with her big brother; he was always ignoring her. She opened a sticky hand and said, 'Look what Khefre gave me.' On her palm lay an oval glass scarab.

Setna frowned. 'You shouldn't have taken it from him. He's only a servant-boy.'

Tiy was good at ignoring things she did not want to hear. 'I have three amulets now,' she said. 'And I want more.'

'Why?'

'Because they're pretty, and I like to collect them.'

'They're not toys, Tiy. They are made to give you the gods' protection when you wear them or pray to them.'

Setna fingered the ankh hanging from his neck. He firmly believed it held the gods' blessings. But he was worried that he hadn't got his other amulet. Had his father noticed?

Left alone with his sister, he soon got fed up. She kept tugging at his hand, forcing him to run this way and that, crying or stamping her foot angrily when he tried to refuse.

Then some of his class mates saw him and started laughing at him.

This was the last straw. Setna went to look for the nurse but he could not find her, and his impatience increased. At last he found a neighbour of theirs. 'Will you look after Tiy for a while. Her nurse is missing and I've got to go.'

He ran to join his classmates before the neighbour could protest, ignoring Tiy's cries to come back.

In high spirits, Setna and his classmates wove in and out of the procession. The barks came to rest at special places along the route, and there was more singing, dancing and prayers. The boys became restless. They went off on their own, found a patch of sand, and held a wrestling contest. Setna managed to reach the final. But then he was up against the toughest boy in his class, and he lost.

'If I'd had my amulet of Hapy,' he muttered to himself, 'I would have won!'

When he went to look for Tiy, he was sticky with dust, sand and sweat, his tunic smeared, his sandals scuffed. She, of course, was nowhere to be found. He pushed through the crowds, shouting her name, afraid of getting told off for losing her. People turned on him, saying he was being disrespectful to the gods.

He had some explaining to do to Nofret, his mother. She was angry with him and anxious about Tiy. After much frantic searching, a servant reported that Tiy had been taken home by the neighbour.

'Never do that again!' Nofret said to him, before she hurried away.

That evening, they all stood on the roof of Setna's uncle's house, not far from the banks of the great river, and watched the waters begin to rise. From that point, it was obvious, even to Tiy, the difference the river made. On the banks there was a thick carpet of bright, green plants. Beyond them, there was nothing but desert.

The children were allowed to join the celebrations in their uncle's house, which was almost as big as their own. He was a rich boat-

11

builder. The tables were weighed down with food. Setna enjoyed himself so much he almost forgot about his lost amulet and the careless way he had treated his sister.

But his father hadn't. In the morning, Khefre came into Setna's room and said, 'Your father wants to see you at once.'

Setna felt nervous. He did not know his father very well - he was often away, painting and carving reliefs in the great temple complex near Thebes. When his father was at home, he was usually out in the fields supervising the planting and harvesting of the crops. He left child-rearing to his wife. He was tall, strong, imposing, and Setna felt very small in his presence.

'I am disappointed in you, Setna,' his father began. 'I had hoped that, at this joyous time, there could be a new beginning for you and I too.'

Setna swallowed hard. What could this mean?

His father reached out and touched the boy's single plait. 'Soon it will be time for you to grow your hair like a man, to leave childish things behind. Your mother and I have been thinking of giving you permission to cut this off.'

Setna's eyes lit up.

'But after what I saw yesterday, I am wondering whether you are ready for it. You accuse a servant-boy of theft without proof. You abandon your sister to a neighbour. And on the very day of inundation, you wrestle in the mud like a common boy. Are these the actions of a sensible youth?'

'No, Father.'

'You are not yet eleven. There is time enough before we cut off your sidelock. I shall be watching how you behave, Setna. Now go, and think about what I have said.'

'Yes, Father.'

When he returned to his room, Setna found Khefre there. 'What are you doing here?' he demanded.

'I'm still looking for your amulet.'

Setna glared at him. Was he telling the truth? But remembering his father's words, he said no more.

'I heard you almost won the wrestling match yesterday,' Khefre said. 'You must be good.'

Setna nodded. 'That was the only good

thing that happened yesterday.'

'I used to wrestle,' Khefre said. 'I could show you some tricks.'

Setna looked at the servant-boy. Was he being friendly, or just making fun of him? He couldn't tell. 'My father wouldn't like me wrestling with a servant-boy,' he said. But both boys knew this wasn't true.

After Khefre had left, Setna thought of his missing amulet. It was surely the cause of his misfortunes. With it, he might have had his sidelock cut at last. Without it, he was still just a boy. Oh how he longed to grow up!

PART TWO

PERET: WHEN THE CROPS GROW

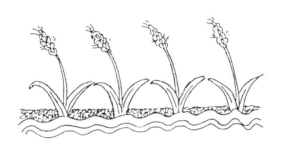

Ever since the visit to the temple at the start of Akhet, Setna had been having strange dreams. One in particular kept recurring.

He was being chased by the god Hapy. The ugly, pot-bellied god, river plants flowing from his head, stomped with heavy feet through the endless pillars of the temple. To escape him, Setna climbed down one of the sacred wells in the first courtyard, only to find himself in the underground caverns where the god lived.

But there he found his amulet. The

minute he touched it, he was transported to the innermost chapel of the temple. Only Pharaoh and his priests were allowed in there. Looking up, he saw the dazzling goddess Ma'at seated high up with a great ostrich feather in her hair. In front of her was a pair of scales. On one side, she weighed his heart, the centre of all wisdom; on the other was a feather. The scales moved slowly up and down, never settling.

He asked his mother, Nofret, what this dream might mean.

'The lost amulet continues to worry you,' she said. 'That is good. And I'm interested that you saw the goddess Ma'at in your dream. She only appears to those who deserve it. What do you think the scales say?'

' I don't know...' Setna struggled to find the right words. 'Perhaps that I'm not as good as I should be?'

Nofret raised her eyebrows and smiled. It was the sort of answer she was hoping for. The boy was growing up! 'Always be fair in what you do and say,' she said. 'And then the scales will balance.'

At school, the boys sometimes sat in the

shade and listened to Siamun tell stories of the old gods. Setna learnt that the body of the god Geb became the earth from which all life - from the lowliest weed to the tallest tree - sprang. The carvings on the temple columns showed this. He learnt that his wife, the goddess Nut, arched over him and became the sky. Her stars glittered on the temple ceiling. 'That's how the world began', said Siamun.

He thrilled to the story of how the great god Osiris was murdered by his brother Set, and of how Osiris's wife Isis brought him back to life and gave birth to their son Horus.

'She was a great queen,' said Siamun. 'She ruled wisely while her son was a child and her husband lived in the Underworld.'

The many hours the boys spent copying out old letters, reports and instructions were much less interesting. They were not written in the beautiful picture language to be found in the temples, but in the lines of shapes across the page, called hieratic script. Setna tried hard not to make mistakes, but he often did. Then Siamun would make him start all over again.

They had to learn a lot by heart, too, and Setna found this the hardest of all. When he stumbled over his words, Siamun would say,

'You waste your time wrestling and at target practice and playing senet.'

'He's the best at knucklebones!' one of the boys interrupted cheekily.

'As a child of your father, you should be the best at learning,' Siamun said sternly. 'Don't you realise your father is one of the Pharaoh's best temple artists? He didn't get that position by playing childish games.'

Setna bowed his head.

'All of you should remember,' said Siamun to the class, 'that most of the boys of this great land of ours never get the chance to learn to read or write or juggle with numbers. At best, they can learn a trade from their fathers or tend the land. And as for the girls ...' He shrugged.

Setna returned to his copying, determined to do better.

Siamun nodded encouragingly when Setna showed him his work. 'Keep up this improvement and one day you might - just might - be one of the boys selected to learn to write the temple language.'

'You mean, hieroglyphics?' He'd often puzzled over the picture language painted on the temple walls, it seemed so mysterious and beautiful. 'I'd love to learn to read and write that!'

'There's no harm in aiming for it. Your father would certainly be pleased.'

'My mother too.'

'Well, there you are then!'

But the minute he got into the courtyard and began kicking a ball around, all thought of working hard to please his parents flew from his mind. The only important thing was to score. And sometimes, because he was so desperate to win, he forgot himself and cheated or fouled.

Only later, at night, or when he was telling Khefre about it, did he feel a little ashamed of himself. Then he would think of the goddess Ma'at. He would bow down to the little image of her placed in the shrine at home and say he was sorry.

Setna never entirely got rid of his suspicion that Khefre had stolen his amulet of Hapy. He felt most sure of it when Khefre beat him at wrestling or archery after school. Surely, being a captive servant-boy with no home of his own, he should let Setna win at least some of the contests?

But as the spring time passed, and Setna became more skillful, he began to see what Khefre was up to. 'You're getting better all the time,' the servant-boy said one day. 'Soon you'll be a match for me.'

Maybe it had been his sister all along. Tiy now had a collection of seven amulets, one for each year of her age. They were made of stone or glass and showed various things - a hand, a cat, a hippopotamus. She had little idea of the protection they gave her. They were just pretty.

Once he crept into her room to search for the missing amulet. His mother caught him doing it. He had to confess his suspicions.

'How can you believe that of your sister?' she said. 'Isn't it more likely that you lost it yourself? Why seek to blame others?'

To try and make amends, he promised Tiy that he would teach her some of the hieratic script he was learning at school. Girls did not go to school. No one else seemed to have the time to teach her. Tiy was overjoyed. Every day, when he came home from school, she pestered him to keep his promise. She caught on quickly, and soon she was able to help him learn his school texts by heart.

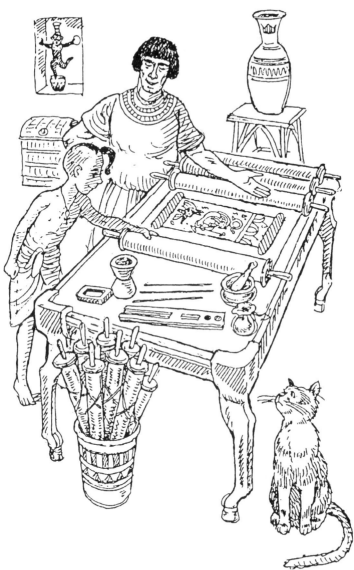

Having overseen the planting of wheat, barley and vegetables on his land, Setna's father had little to do until harvest time. This was the season when he went away to help decorate the pharaoh's great temple near Thebes. Setna's mother ran the house while he was away, and saw to all his affairs, but everyone missed him.

On the night before he was to leave, Salitis called his son to his workshop. On the table were scrolls of drawings he had made. 'These are designs I have drawn for the walls and columns in the great hall at the temple of Ipet-isut,' he said proudly. 'Do you know what that means?'

Setna shook his head.

'It means 'The Most Perfect Place.' And it is.'

'Is it far?'

'No, just down river, on the bank opposite Luxor. King Seti is building a great hall dedicated to the god Amun. It will have 134 huge columns - much bigger than the ones in our own temple. And the columns will have carvings showing the Creation.'

Setna looked more closely at the drawings. They showed flowers and papyrus plants, animal and bird-headed gods.

'I hope to persuade King Seti to allow them to be carved on some of the great pillars,' said his father.

'I wish I could see the temple,' said Setna.

He was astounded when his father said, 'You shall.'

Wide-eyed, he said, 'I shall?'

'Your mother and I agree that you have become more sensible since the festival of inundation. We have noticed that you show more respect to Khefre, that you are not too proud to learn from him. We are pleased that you are teaching your sister to read and write. And Siamun says you are trying harder at school. You have taken the right path since I spoke to you about this before. I shall be glad to take you.'

It was on the tip of Setna's tongue to say, 'And can I have my plait cut off? Can I grow my hair like the older boys?' But instinct made him keep quiet.

The following morning, while he was packing a few belongings, Khefre stood by the door, waiting respectfully. In his excitement, Setna ignored him until he saw the strange look on the servant-boy's face.

'What's the matter?' he said. 'Are you sorry to see me go?'

'I shall miss our wrestling matches and archery contests. But I have something else to tell you.'

'What is it? You'll have to hurry. I can't

keep Father waiting.'

'This morning Tiy came to me. She was worried. Too worried to speak to you herself. So she asked me to.'

'I don't understand. Worried about what? I shall be perfectly safe where I'm going.'

'About this.' Khefre stepped forward and opened his hand. In it lay Setna's missing amulet of the god Hapy.

Setna snatched it. 'I always knew you took it!' he shouted, his surprise turning to anger.

'No, not me,' Khefre stammered. 'You misunderstand me. Your sister ... she took it and she...'

'Don't you dare try to blame Tiy for this!' It was one thing for *him* to think it - quite another for a servant-boy.

'But it was...' Khefre protested. 'She didn't mean anything by it. She just wanted you to have it back for your trip.'

Setna glared at the servant-boy. 'How dare you! If I wasn't about to leave, I'd see that you were dismissed for this. Now get out of my sight.'

Khefre looked shocked. He slunk out.

Setna hung the amulet around his neck. 'I'll deal with him when I get back,' he thought.

'He won't get away with this.'

He tried to feel good about how he had behaved, but in his heart he was troubled. Over the last few months, Khefre had almost become a friend. Still, he had his amulet back, and that was what really mattered.

Setna and his father travelled down the Nile in one of his uncle's swift boats, keeping near enough to the bank to see the rich green crops in the sunlight. Sometimes, Setna was allowed to help steer the ship.

They sat under a canopy watching the oarsmen heave back and forth, sweating.

'So you found your amulet at last,' his father observed.

'Yes,' Setna answered. He flushed.

'Where was it?'

'Khefre had it.'

Salitis looked surprised. 'All this time?'

Setna shrugged as if to say, 'What do you expect of a servant-boy?'

'I hope you are sure of this, Setna,' his father said gravely. 'Accusing someone of a crime they did not commit would offend the goddess Ma'at. She weighs all such judgements.'

Setna's flush deepened. But he thought to himself, 'Surely it is worse to think it was my sister?'

They arrived at the temple complex. Turning into a narrow channel, they entered a small harbour where their ship was anchored. Setna followed behind his father as they walked up a long dusty avenue. On each side were palm trees and statues of ram-headed sphinxes. They came to a great wall and the first huge gate.

'There are many temples here,' his father explained. 'Each of the pharaohs seeks to improve what their forefathers have done. King Seti is building a great hall with many columns, dedicated to the god Amun.'

They passed through the first gate into a courtyard, and then through another one. There were giant paintings of the god Amun on the walls of the gate, and smaller paintings showing the pharaoh crushing his enemies. Pennants fluttered high on poles fixed inside grooves in the walls.

Once through the second gate, they came into the half-finished hall of giant pillars. Its sheer size took Setna's breath away. It was so much bigger than the temple at home. Many craftsmen were working on carvings in the hall.

Salitis was welcomed by several foremen. He showed them his drawings.

'You must take them to the king yourself,' they said.

Salitis suddenly looked nervous. 'King Seti is here?'

'He is here with his wife and youngest son. He comes every day to supervise us. He will be glad to meet you.'

Salitis turned to Setna. 'I will find a servant to take you to the house where we shall be staying. Wait there for me.'

'Yes, Father.'

Setna watched his father recede into the temple, clutching his scroll of drawings. To think that his father was about to meet the pharaoh! What would the boys back home say about that?

Following a servant-woman, Setna travelled through bright courtyards, past huge obelisks and statues of the gods, into an area where there were many houses.

'This is the house you will be staying in while you're here,' said the servant.

There were three main rooms, the largest with a pillar in the middle of it. There was a courtyard where the cooking was done, and a cellar where the wine was kept. It did not take

Setna long to look round.

He climbed up to the roof. From there he could see how huge the whole place was. In front of him were all the main buildings, a shimmering lake, palm trees, houses, the great wall. Despite what his father had said, he had to get out and explore!

He soon got lost. Obelisk after obelisk towered so high he was blinded by the sunlight when he tried to look up at them. Gate after gate, each with wonderful carved paintings of gods and pharaohs. There were busy workshops, food stores, animal pens. Everywhere, there were workmen, servants, animals. And everywhere was the noise of the building works as King Seti's workmen added to the glory of the place.

Setna was puzzling over the hieroglyphics on the huge double walls of the ninth gate, when a voice behind him said, 'Can't you read those?'

He turned and saw a boy of about his own age, his hair still in a plait. The boy looked proud and richly dressed, but there was a lively amusement in his eyes. Setna thought, 'This boy belongs in this place, in a way that I don't.'

'Where I come from,' Setna explained,

'only a few older boys are taught this language. But I want to learn it.'

'Why?'

'Because it's beautiful.'

'Is that all?'

'No. It's full of mystery, isn't it?'

'Yes! Songs and prayers and riddles and instructions and stories of the gods. It is the language of the gods. Are you good enough to learn it?'

'Yes!' Setna declared. 'Are you?'

The boy smiled, as if this was a joke.

'I'm Rameses,' he said. 'Call me Ra. My father is here, too, supervising work in the temple. Is your father working in the temple?'

Setna nodded.

'I thought so,' said Ra. 'While they work, shall we play? I can show you around, if you like.'

They passed through another huge gateway. The scene that opened up before Setna stopped him in his tracks. Stretching down to another smaller temple - 'That's the temple of Mut,' Ra said - was a long avenue of huge stone sphinxes. Half-lion, half-ram, they crouched like monsters either side of the boys, their paws stretched towards them.

'Come on,' Ra shouted. 'Let's climb over

them!'

'But you can't,' Setna protested. 'It isn't allowed, is it?'

'I can do anything I want,' Ra laughed. 'And as you're my friend, you can too.'

They climbed the stone monsters. They wove in and out of them, their voices echoing between the stones. No one tried to stop them. In fact, when they saw Ra they all smiled or bowed. Who was this boy, Setna wondered. He must be someone quite important.

Once inside the temple of Mut, Ra grew quiet. He pointed to a statue of the goddess. She had the head of a lioness. 'She is the daughter of the great sun-god,' Ra explained. 'She is his ears and eyes.'

'Who's this, then?' Setna asked, pointing to another statue. It showed a goddess in a brightly coloured dress, wearing a headress of vulture feathers on top of a white crown.

'That is Mut too. She has more than one form. She protects the king, like a mother. One day, she will protect me.'

Further in the temple, they came across a wall painting. It showed the goddess Ma'at with her scales.

'Why are you staring at her like that?' asked Ra.

'Because I dream of her. Her scales with my heart in them are never still.'

'Have you done wrong, then?'

Setna looked at Ra sadly. 'I believe that I accused my friend the Nubian servant-boy of stealing an amulet when he didn't.'

'Then the scales will not balance. This is the goddess of justice. She weighs what you do and judges you. You must put it right. You will never have peace in the after-life if you don't.'

'But I shall look such a fool!'

'Aren't you strong enough for that?'

'I don't know,' said Setna.

Setna joined the local school and made new friends there.

He was happy to have his father to himself during the evenings. They got to know each other as they had never done before.

In the days and weeks that followed, he never knew when his mysterious new friend Ra would turn up and insist he come out to play. The boy did not go to the school, and yet he was well-educated. He taught Setna some of the picture language so that he could read what was written on the temple walls and obelisks.

To cool down, they often swam in the sacred lakes. These were used only by the priests, and Setna thought it odd that no one else - let alone the other boys - swam there too. But it seemed that there was something magic about Ra. Everyone let him do as he pleased.

Setna's father often came back home with tales of how wise and clever King Seti was. But Setna never expected to meet the pharaoh. Then, one day, all that changed.

Hot and dusty after a hard day at school, he went to the lake half-surrounding the temple of Mut and waited there for Ra. His friend often turned up at that time of day. But there was no sign of him.

Setna couldn't wait any longer. He slipped out of his loin cloth and plunged into the waters. Never had the lake felt so good. Floating on his back, the sun burning red through his eyelids, he did not at first hear the shouts from the bank. But when he looked, he saw two shaven-headed priests in white robes gesturing angrily to him to get out of the water. As he swam towards them, he wondered what he had done wrong.

They seized him by the arms and shouted at him. 'This is a sacred lake. It is for priests only, not for common boys'.

'But I often swim here,' he protested. 'You've seen me.'

'Only because you were with the son of the divine king. Without his presence, you are nothing.'

Setna did not understand. Bewildered, he bowed his head while they continued to tell him off.

Then suddenly, they were silent.

Looking up, Setna saw a man approach, dressed in a rich robe and jewellery. With a shock, he recognised the pharaoh, walking with some courtiers. Trembling, he fell to his knees.

'What is happening here?' King Seti asked.

The priests explained.

'Ah, so you are the boy Rameses has taken so much to heart.' The king studied Setna with interest. 'Arise. You are not in disgrace.'

Setna rose uncertainly.

'My son has often talked about his new friend Setna,' the king said. 'You have taught him so much, although you may not know it.'

Setna gazed at him. Rameses? His son?

Did that mean...? He shivered, although the sun was burning on his quickly drying skin.

King Seti turned to the priests. 'Let us hear no more of this. The boy was at fault, but he was not to know. You can see that he is repentant.'

The pharaoh patted Setna's head, smiled, and continued on his way.

As soon as he had gone, the priests scowled at Setna. They shooed him away with a few harsh words, making it clear that he'd had more luck that he deserved.

Setna hurried home. His head was burning, his eyes full of the pharaoh. And he was bewildered. Ra, the pharaoh's son? Why hadn't his friend said so? Why let him believe all this time that he was just an ordinary boy, the son of an overseer?

'But if he had told you,' said his father, 'could you still have played with him? You would have been too awed. You would not have been yourself.'

'Did you know, Father?'

His father chuckled. 'Of course I did! It amused me that you never saw it. And it made me proud, too.'

When Ra sought him out later that evening, Setna no longer saw his friend. He saw instead the son of the great pharaoh, one day to be king himself. He stammered and blushed and did not know what to say. What an idiot he felt!

Ra understood at once what had happened. 'It was good while it lasted,' he sighed. 'Don't blame me for not telling you. I just wanted to play like the other boys, and you let me do that. We're still friends, aren't we?'

Setna nodded. But he knew they could never be friends in quite the same way again.

'I hear you're going home soon,' Ra said.

'Yes,' Setna replied, finding his voice at last. 'The harvest will be starting soon. My father supervises that, and I like to help him.'

'When you come again next year, you won't forget me, will you?'

'How could I? We've had great fun, the best ever!'

'We have. And look, I've brought you something.'

He handed over a little parcel wrapped in papyrus. Inside it was a golden amulet of the goddess Ma'at. She was shown seated with an ostrich feather rising from her headgear. There was a pair of scales in her hands.

'Wear it and be fair to everyone you meet,' said Ra.

PART THREE

SHEMU: HARVEST TIME

Setna was so full of himself, as soon as he got home he said to his mother, 'Surely I am grown up enough now to have my sidelock cut off.' He tugged at his plait in disgust.

'Your father has given good reports of you. Maybe it is time. But let us wait until your name day, shall we? It's only a month away. You will be eleven then, the same age as your father and uncle when they had their sidelocks cut.'

Setna jumped up and down with pleasure.

'But until then...' his mother warned.

The minute Tiy saw the amulet of Ma'at

she begged to have it. She admired it, clutched it, pleaded for it, even shed tears, hoping he would give it to her.

'Prince Ra gave it to me,' he said, tugging it away from her. 'Nothing will make me give it away. I shall keep it by my side all my life!'

At school, he could not help boasting of his friendship with Prince Ra. He told his classmates how they had explored the temple grounds, climbed over sphinxes, swum in the sacred lakes. At first, they listened with awe. But after a few days, his stories grew stale, and they listened with less interest. Before long the stories became more and more like boasts. The boys did not like that. Setna was growing big-headed!

'Don't you talk about anything else?' they complained.

'*You* weren't singled out by the pharaoh's son,' he retorted. 'You're jealous! All of you!'

He became proud. The boys pushed him away from their games. They laughed at him behind his back.

Siamun soon noticed what was going on. 'Why do you think Prince Rameses chose you to be his friend?' he asked.

'Because he liked me.'

'Of course he did. But *why* did he like you?'

Setna shrugged. How could he answer a question like that?

'It's because with him you were always yourself. *Your better self.* In his company, you couldn't be anything else. You didn't boast, did you? Or show off, or point the finger at others? You didn't bow and scrape to him, like some would. Think about it, Setna.'

Setna looked puzzled.

'What would he think of you now, boasting and putting on airs?'

Setna held his amulet tight in his hand and said nothing.

On the way home, some of the boys strutted around him, their noses in the air, pretending to be princes. 'Really, how common everyone is!' they declared, mockingly.

'Go away!' Setna shouted.

They teased him until he was ready to hit them. They ran away, laughing at his red and angry face.

When he arrived home, he saw Khefre rolling a jug across the courtyard.

'I want to wrestle,' Setna demanded.

'As soon as I've moved this,' Khefre said.

'No, now!' Setna shouted.

Khefre paused and wiped his brow. 'Did the prince teach you some new holds?'

'You'll see.'

'You should calm down first. It's not good to fight in that mood.'

'Are you afraid to fight me now?'

'If that's what you want,' said Khefre, smiling grimly.

They locked arms. Setna's anger made him try harder than ever before. Several times Khefre seemed to be in a hold he could not possibly escape. But then somehow he would be free, standing there grinning as if to say, 'You'll never pin me down for long!'

The match ended in a draw. Setna had the suspicion that Khefre could have won if he had wanted to. It made him boil with rage. Why, since he came home, did no one take him seriously? Why did no one treat him like Ra had done?

Siamun came to the house. Setna knew he would tell his parents about his boastful behaviour at school. His parents would think twice now about letting him wear his hair long like the other boys.

It was time for the crops to be gathered in.

'Setna, I hope you will help with the

harvest again this year,' his father said. 'One day, you will be the overseer of these lands. You must learn everything there is to know about farming.'

'Of course, Father.' It would be a relief to get away from the boys at school for a while and to do something to please his parents.

'Can I come too?' Tiy asked.

'The harvesting is for men and boys,' Setna said in a superior voice. 'You'd only get in the way.' But the minute he had said that, he saw the frown on his mother's face.

'I'll take you down later,' she said to Tiy, 'when the women start winnowing.'

Setna placed his precious amulet of the goddess Ma'at in an alcove beside the one of Hapy. 'Look after these while I'm in the fields,' he said to Khefre. 'I'm frightened I shall lose them down there.'

'But I'm going too,' said Khefre. 'As soon as I've finished here. Your father said.'

'Oh, well, I expect they'll be safe.'

The boys travelled out of the town and down to the fields stretching along the Nile. They walked around the fields, along dykes by the side of the canals, to get to the land harvested by Setna's father. Here, a row of men were advancing slowly in a line, cutting the head of the corn with their sickles of flint. They threw handfuls of corn behind them as they progressed.

The boys joined the women and children behind the men. They gathered the corn into large baskets and helped carry them on poles to the threshing floor. They worked together all day without arguing. Setna thought, this was how it used to be between Khefre and me before I went away. Like friends. He was glad now that he hadn't said anything more about the missing amulet.

Nofret brought Tiy down to watch the threshing. Oxen and donkeys trampled on the corn to separate the ears from the stalks. Then women threw the ears into the air. The breeze from the wooden fans waved by the women blew away the chaff, and the grain fell.

Salitis joined them for lunch under the shade of vines. They had bread, figs, honey and beer. 'Once all this has been harvested, we shall plant vegetables and flax,' he said. 'There should be time for them to grow before the next inundation. I want you to watch how they are planted, Setna. Have a go at planting them yourself. Learn everything you can.'

Setna noticed that Tiy kept looking at him

in a funny way. What was she up to now?

On the way home that evening, Khefre said, 'Your father must be very rich to own all this land. My father farmed no more than a patch. There was never enough for us to eat.'

Setna could have let Khefre go on believing that, and for a minute he said nothing. But he had enjoyed the boy's company that day. It had reminded him of his friendship with Ra.

'No, Khefre, you don't understand' he said. 'All this land belongs to the temple, and we farm it for the pharaoh. It's all his, really. We keep some of the harvest for ourselves, but the rest goes to the temple to be eaten or sold. At least your father owned his own field. We don't own any of this!'

Khefre gave him a wondering look.

'Race you back home!' he said suddenly.

For once, Setna did not mind losing.

Once he had bathed and changed his tunic, he thought he would give thanks to Ma'at for a good day.

But his precious amulet wasn't there in the alcove. He stared at the empty place where he had placed it that morning. He had a sinking feeling in the pit of his stomach. Khefre! No the boy had been with him all day.

Besides, he now admitted to himself that Khefre would never do such a thing. Tiy, then. Who else could it be?

He looked out of the window and saw Khefre crossing the courtyard. He called to him.

'My amulet is missing. The one Prince Rameses gave me.'

Khefre looked uneasy. 'You don't think it was me?'

'No, Khefre, I don't think it was you. And I want to say sorry to you for once thinking you stole the one of Hapy. I couldn't bear to think it had been taken by my sister.'

'Do you think she's taken this one too?'

'Let's go and ask her.'

They found Tiy playing with her amulets. She had them all lined up on the floor. The boys stood quietly either side of her. She looked up, and a guilty expression covered her face.

'Where is it, Tiy?' Setna said softly; there was no point in being angry. 'You know what I mean.'

Tiy was about to protest her innocence, but then she saw the look on her brother's face. Without a word, she fished the amulet from under her bedclothes and handed it over to him with a little sigh.

Setna smiled, relieved to have it back. 'I shall say nothing about this Tiy, if you don't.' She looked at him in surprise.

'When you learn that these amulets are not just toys, you won't take them again.' He held up the amulet. 'You see, I pray to the goddess Ma'at, ever since I saw her in the temple with Ra. She helps me get things right.'

'Can I pray to her too?'

'She'll always be in my room, in the alcove where I keep the amulet of Hapy too. You can pray to her there, if you want.'

Once the harvest was in, and the first of the new crops planted, Setna returned to school. He hoped that in his absence his classmates would have forgotten his boasting. He wondered how he could make amends. His name-day was only a week away and he wanted it to be a new beginning not just at home but at school too.

The boys no longer laughed at him. But neither did they include him in their games. They just ignored him. He didn't protest or pretend it wasn't happening, or try to barge his way into their games. He went quietly about his business. He helped others with their work when he could. He held back when Siamun asked questions, to give others a chance of answering. He kept his head down and worked hard.

On the day before his name-day, Siamun took him aside. 'I have a letter here from a teacher at the school at Ipet-isut. Prince Ra commanded him to write to me.'

'Prince Ra?' His heart leapt. 'What about?'

'He asks that you be taught the language of the temples.'

'The beautiful picture language?' Setna said excitedly. 'And can I?'

'I have the prince's command. You should be proud of yourself, Setna. Some god is keeping a special eye on you.'

Setna felt his pride rising. Then he remembered. His smile faded. 'You won't tell the others, will you? They'd say it wasn't fair.'

'If that is what you want.'

'What I want,' said Setna slowly, 'is to do what I'm best at. If that means painting hieroglyphics, fine. But if I'm not good enough...' He shrugged.

But all day he went about with a little

glow inside him. Ra hadn't forgotten him. They would still be friends.

On the morning of his name-day, Setna spent a few quiet minutes in his room praying to the amulet of the goddess Ma'at. He closed his eyes and saw the scales in her hand, his heart one side, a feather the other. The scales were perfectly balanced. He kept his eye on them and they did not stir. He knew that in the months ahead, the scales would dip and rise again, but today they would be in balance.

A friend of his father's, a priest, came to their house. Setna was seated in his father's special chair. All around him stood his family. Khefre joined them at his request. Nofret held up a polished disk of metal so that he could look into it and see what was happening.

'I know you have waited a long time for this moment,' said Salitis. 'We have all noticed, lately, how grown up you've become, almost a man. The time has come to cut off your sidelock. You may grow your hair like Khefre's!'

With a little flourish of his scissors, the priest approached Setna. They watched in

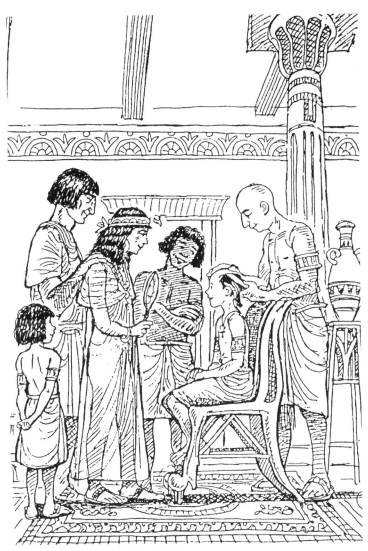

silence as he sliced through the plait.

    Setna felt some hidden weight fall from
him as the plait fell to the floor. He took the
mirror and gazed at himself. How bare his

head looked!

'What's the matter now?' Nofret smiled.

'How long will I have to wait before my hair grows?'

'Oh, months, I expect. The inundation will be here and gone before it'll be fully grown!'

Setna groaned. Everyone laughed.

He was given gifts - a writing set, rolls of papyrus to practise on, a necklace of blue and amber beads, some fine sandals. Khefre gave him a carving of a bull that he had made himself.

That night, after the party for his name-day, he went to his room, sat on his bed, and looked at his two amulets. He gave thanks to Hapy for the river that watered the land and made his life so comfortable. And he gave thanks to Ma'at for showing him how to behave.

Then he smoothed out a roll of papyrus on the table, dipped the nib of his new pen in ink, and began his first letter to Prince Ra. He told him of all the things that had happened to him since they had parted at the end of Peret - the harvest, the teasing at school, making friends with Khefre. 'I shall always try to keep Ma'at's scales balanced,' he wrote.

'It's hard at times, but it makes me feel better.'

He ended by saying, 'And when you next see me, you'll find me with a fine head of thick black hair. Will yours be like that too?'

Glossary

Ankh: a hieroglyphic sign meaning 'life'. It took the form of a T-shape surmounted by a loop. When, in hieroglyphics, it is offered by the gods to a pharaoh, it means he is being given eternal life.

Amulets: small objects worn on the body as a charm. They were thought to protect the wearer from disease and danger. They showed gods, animals, parts of the body: the variety was huge.

Hapy: a god who represented the Nile inundation on which so much of life at that time depended.

House of Life: part of the temple buildings where priests, scribes and boys were trained to read and write and where texts were copied. Most learnt a pictureless script called hieratic. A few went on to learn to write in symbols, i.e. heiroglyphics.

Children: most boys did not learn to read or

write but learned a trade, usually from their fathers. A few boys of rich families, like Setna, would attend the House of Life to learn reading, writing and mathematics. Girls would learn housecraft and help with the harvest.

Ipet-isut: a huge temple complex near Thebes, now known as Karnak.

Ma'at: the goddess who represented truth, justice and balance in nature. But the *idea* of Ma'at was much larger than this: she also represented divine order throughout the world.

Name-day: similar to a birthday. Names were regarded as a living part of each human being; without them, it was thought new-born babies could not properly come into the world as full human beings.

Pharaoh: he (all but two were men) were considered to be gods as well as kings.

Prince Rameses: (ruled 1279-1213 BC): son to **King Seti I** (ruled 1294-1279), became Rameses II. His reign was long and was noted for the vast number of temples, monuments and statuary built during his time.

The seasons: the year was divided into three main seasons, each lasting four months. Months were thirty days long (leaving five days in the year outside the seasons). The first season was called **Akhet**, coinciding with the Nile inundation. The second was called **Peret**, when the crops grew. The last was called **Shemu**, when the crops were harvested.

Sidelock of youth: all children were thought to have thier hair shaven one side, tied into a plait on the other, until they reached the age of ten or eleven, when they were allowed to cut off thier sidelock and grow thier hair.

Senet: a game, newly invented at the time of the story, in which pegs are moved around an oblong board consisting of thirty squares (10 x 3).

Sistrum: a musical rattling instrument usually played by women.

Temples: the larger ones had many chapels dedicated to different gods. There would be an inner chapel dedicated to the main god of the temple, such as Amum or Ma'at. Some also had a hyperstyle hall consisting of many giant columns. Only priests, representing the pharaoh, were allowed in the inner chapels, important families in the outer ones. The ordinary mass of people would not be allowed beyond the first court, if at all. Offerings of food and other gifts were made daily to the gods.

Servants and slaves: people like Khefre were captured in wars against other nations and brought back to be sold into slavery or adopted as servants.